THE
CLUB
THROWER'S
HANDBOOK

Throwing Golf Clubs
For Distance & Accuracy

Double Eagle
Press

THE
CLUB
THROWER'S
HANDBOOK

*Throwing Golf Clubs
For Distance & Accuracy*

Tom Carey

First published March 13, 1995

Manufactured in the United States of America
ISBN: 1-877590-91-6

Published by
Double Eagle Press
1247 W. Wellington
Chicago, IL 60657

This book is dedicated to the 87% of golfers who admit to having ever thrown a club.

And to the 13% who lied about it.

TABLE OF CONTENTS

A LIST OF OUR ADVERTISERS

We are happy to recommend the following fine products and hope that you will patronize our advertisers.

Heave 'em & Leave 'em:
An Introduction

I love golf. I say this proudly. I have worn alpaca. I have worn Sans-A-Belts. I have worn shoes with a frilly little flap on them. I subscribe to "Golf Magazine", "Golf Digest", "Golf World", "Golf Tips", "Golf Illustrated", "Golf Tips Illustrated", "World Of Golf Illustrated Magazine & Digest" and "Playboy". (But only for the golf articles).

Neither rain, nor sleet, nor snow, nor gloom of night has ever kept me from my appointed round of golf. Especially if I had a guaranteed tee time.

And ... I throw my clubs. I toss them like a salad, heave them like last night's tequila shooters and kick them like a bad habit. And I'm proud of it. If you throw your clubs (and I'm sure you do, or how else would come to possess this book?) you should be proud of it, too. Club throwing is an art. It relieves stress, burns calories, builds muscle and it keeps all the other players on the golf course on their toes.

This book is for those golfers who have never quite been able to control their tempers. Those whose only relief after a terrible shot comes when the offending club is soaring skyward or rattling across some parking lot throwing sparks as it goes.

By virtue of the handbook and bag tag now in your hands, you have officially become a member in good standing of the Club Throwers of America. There are no dues to pay and no meetings to attend. I know you need every cent for new clubs and higher insurance premiums. Just having another golfer in the brotherhood of Club Throwers is enough for me. (Though the dough I got for the book is nice, too).

So clap that bag tag on the old Hot-Z and head on out to your favorite track. Tee it up and let it fly. And when that tee ball does a major right-to-right on you, loft your driver after it. If it ends up on the clubhouse roof, well, so be it. Smile proudly at the outraged members marching across the fairway toward you and say, "I'm a Club Thrower. We heave 'em and leave 'em."

Throwing Clubs
For Distance & Accuracy

Just as there is a right way and a wrong way to swing a golf club, there is a right way and a wrong way to *throw* a golf club. These instructions are to guide you, the proud and happy Club Thrower, in the fine art of "implement levitation."

The Two-Handed Method

This is far and away (hmm, far and away, nice choice of words) the most popular club heaving style among players today. But many fail to achieve the kind of distance or accuracy that is necessary for a truly "elevating" experience. The following will help you get the most out of every club (and tantrum) you throw.

1. Take the club back in a flat arc, parallel to the ground. A good shoulder turn is very important to get the lift you need.

2. Begin the forward swing with a quick turn of the front shoulder and step toward the target. Keeping the arms extended, release the club at about eye level. This will impart a counter-clockwise spin (for righties) and insure maximum carry.

Some tossers find that a grunt or scream such as "Take that you useless piece of crap!" is helpful.

3. Follow through by stepping toward the target. Watch the flight of the club carefully and, if necessary, warn other players of the incoming missile with the traditional cry of "Hey, you guys, look out!"

The "Slam Dunk" Method

Many of the club-throws players use require the club to slam into something; the ground, a ball washer, the ranger, whatever. These "throws" can be dangerous because of the sudden jolt to the player's musco-skeletal system when the club contacts its target. Flying pieces of wood, steel and flesh can also be hazardous. The following will help you minimize physical risk and maximize the havoc you can wreak.

1. Take the club back in a smooth, one-piece motion. Try to get a full extension.

2. Keep the elbows firm, but not locked, during the downswing and all the way through impact. If executed properly, the offending club will bury in the ground or shatter into pieces with a satisfying snap.

Historical Heavers:
Club Throwing's Colorful Past

Golf was invented one typically dark, rainy after-
noon in St. Andrews, Scotland by Olde Tom Morris
and his son, Young Tom Morris. (The Scots are noto-
riously unimaginative when it comes to naming their
kids.) They were spending their day as usual, hang-
ing out by the Loch Ness with their cameras, waiting
for the monster to appear, when a bored Young Tom
absentmindedly took a swipe at a stone on the beach
with his walking stick.

As fate would have it, the stone flew straight at
an old gnarled oak tree some distance away. As they
walked up to the tree, Olde Tom said to his son, "I'll
bet ye five bob ye kin noot strike the tree wi' another
stroke."

Though the rock lay just three feet from the tree,
Young Tom began to shake and sweat from the pres-
sure of the wager and, of course, he missed the putt.

Young Tom was furious. He smashed his walking stick against the tree again and again until it broke. Then he picked up the pieces and threw them into the sea screaming, "It's the devil's oon game we've invented and I'll ne'er play it agin!"

That is how Young Tom Morris invented the yips and Olde Tom Morris invented the Nassau. And, not incidentally, the game of golf. And, of course, club throwing.

They bought new sticks and were back out on the beach again the next day, swinging and swearing and throwing their clubs around. And to this day club throwing remains an integral part of the great game of golf.

GATOR BAIT
Club Throwing Schools

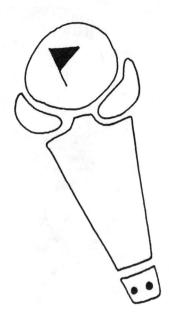

At the Gator Bait Club Throwing Schools you'll enjoy comfortable accommodations in a beautiful condo overlooking Swampgrass National Golf Course, enjoy excellent food and have plenty of time to relax by the pool. You'll receive instruction from the finest teaching pros. Soon you'll be throwing your clubs higher, farther and with more style than ever before. Tuition starts at just $1995* for the three day package and includes lodging, food, green fees, lessons and videotape.

Dial 1-800-THROW IT

Gator Bait Club Throwing Schools
808 Pottawatami Trail   Swampgrass, FL 33407

*Double occupancy. Tax, gratuities and insurance coverage additional.

WHAT'S THE RULE?

Bob tees it up on a long par four and hits a wild slice that could be out of bounds. Naturally, he flings his driver in disgust. Unfortunately, the wayward wand caroms off a bench, snaps in two and a piece of graphite shrapnel pierces the thigh of Bob's playing partner, Jim.

Jim collapses to the ground screaming, blood spurting from his femoral artery. He falls in such a way as cover the entire teeing area. Bob is unable to retee within the tee box to hit his provisional ball what with all the gushing blood and thrashing about. What is the ruling in this situation?

Rule 38-3d states that *"Anytime a player has been grievously injured during play he may be declared an "immovable obstruction". Players may take a drop two club lengths from the nearest point of relief, no closer to the hole."*

Bob may elect to drop just behind or to the side of Jim and play his provisional ball. This will be his third stroke. If he finds his first ball, of course, he may play it with no penalty.

He may also take the time to apply a tourniquet to Jim's leg with the remaining piece of his driver and perhaps move Jim's body into a shady area. Bob must be sure to call the paramedics at his earliest opportunity, either at the halfway house or immediately after putting out at 18.

In match play, Jim loses any hole he is physically unable to complete. In stroke play he incurs a two stroke penalty for every pint of blood spilled on the course.

If he has completed at least nine holes, Jim must report his score to the handicap committee before going to the emergency room.

Shhhh!

Next time you're tip-toeing through someone's
tulips in search of a club you tossed there,
you'll be glad you wore Tip-Toes by
Happy Feet Golf Shoes!

Our patented buffalo hide uppers are made to
hug your little trespassing tootsies like a pair of
moccasins. And they still deliver the support
you need to run fast and hurdle fences when
Fido finds you poking around his yard.

Club Tossing:
An Interlude

You tee the ball up on a bright, sunny morning with the promise of 18 beautiful, unblemished holes stretched out before you. You gaze down at the smooth, clean scorecard which could (who knows?!) in just four short hours hold evidence of a par. Or two. Maybe a birdie! Maybe (dare I say it?) you'll shoot your handicap!

You take your practice swing. Then a waggle or two. Or eight. A slow backswing and pow, a solid hit. You watch the ball begin its flight and then curve, ever so gently out of bounds. Still, all is not lost. Calmly, you retee and swing. Bananaville. Then a worm burner, a couple of pop-ups, a shank and a chilly-dip and, finally, you're on the green.

Your first putt is thirty feet straight uphill. You leave it short by five feet. Firm, then, you think, to the back of the cup. And you roll it two feet past.

As you step up to tap in, your partners have a

31

what seems to be a sudden attack of lockjaw. Surely they don't expect you to putt this? But there is nothing but the sound of the birds in the trees. OK, no problem. You line it up, carefully stroke the ball and watch as it veers off a spike mark, hits the lip, does a 360 and stays out.

Somehow, you remain calm. And then, one of your opponents says it.

"That's good."

That's what does it. That smug, condescending tone of voice. You look down at the putter in your hands. And you do what you must do. You rear back and heave it. And that club flies high and far, end-over-end and out of bounds. And you relax. And your playing partners come out from under cover and you stroll casually to the next tee thinking, "Hell, I'll probably putt better with my two-iron anyway."

Club Toss

Golfwear For The Club Throwing Man

Our quality golf shirts are tailored especially for the club throwing fanatic with a roomy comfortable cut, double stitched seams and extra-long "no pull-out" tail.

Our colors are custom blended to camouflage you when you have to go into someone's yard to retrieve a club. We've treated the all-cotton fabric with Wet-Guard so when you have to wade into a water hazard or duck a sprinkler to pick up the pieces of your five-iron your Club Toss will stay dry!

Now available at your pro shop!

On The Beach

So many players are intimidated when faced with a difficult sand shot. Chances are they'll take two or three tries before throwing the ball out in disgust. A perfect opportunity to throw a club? You bet. However, some precautions must be taken to insure a satisfying club throwing experience when you're "on the beach."

Equipment

If you don't have a sand wedge, get one. This handy club is lofted, flanged and weighted to fly perfectly, end-over-end when tossed from a bunker. If you prefer to bury it up to the grip with a resounding overhead smash it will sink deep into the sand.

It is very important to have a pair of good golf shoes when throwing clubs from the sand. Spiked or spikeless, these shoes will allow you to get solid footing where you otherwise might slip.

36

To do your best in the sand, follow these tips!

One: Take a wider stance than normal with feet, hips, knees and shoulders aimed well left of the target.

Two: Draw the club back as usual, remembering to keep your lower body "quiet."

Three: As you bring the club forward to release it, stride toward your target. Following through with a snap of the wrist will ensure maximum height and club flight. Your sand wedge should bury where ever it lands.

Yes, the sand can be intimidating but with practice and the right equipment you should be able to heave a club just as far from the sand as you can from a nice lie in the fairway.

Distance & Accuracy

You get both with the new *Whirlybird* woods and irons from Airborne Golf. These gravity-balanced, cavity-backed drop forged irons fly higher and farther than any clubs you've ever thrown before. And our perimeter-weighted metal woods have the largest sweet spot ever. Bang them on your cart or beat them on the ballwasher, these beauties can take it!

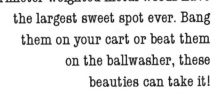

But don't just take our word for it!
Go to your local pro shop and slam a few against the wall. You'll switch to *Whirlybirds* too!

Airborne Golf Clubs

U.S. Patent 6,678,003

Club Throwing Q&A

Q. Isn't throwing your club an unsafe thing to do?

A. Not if it's done properly! Novice club throwers can cause lots of damage to the course and to their playing partners, but for those heavers who have been around awhile it's safety first!

Always throw your club forward! You'll get a clear look at club line of flight, be able to warn any players who might be in danger and you'll be able to pick the club up as you walk by. If you toss a club backwards you'll just have to run back to get it.

It's important to warm up thoroughly before you throw any clubs to avoid back strain and pulled muscles. (See Let's Work Out! on page 48).

Q. I've never thrown a club before. How do I get started on the right foot?

A. Always start your club throwing with some practice time at the range. More and more driving ranges

The Club Thrower's Handbook

these days offer club throwing areas where you can rent a bag of clubs (usually about $5 for a large bag) and practice heaving them.

Warm up with a few short throws. Toss a couple of wedges and putters. Then as your muscles begin to loosen up, begin to throw the longer and heavier clubs working your way gradually up to the woods.

After you get the hang of it you may want to add some cursing and swearing. Veteran club tossers find that a few well chosen screams add immeasurably to the enjoyment they get when throwing clubs.

Q. Can women throw clubs as well as men?

A. Why not! Women may lose some distance in their club throwing, of course, but what they lack in upper body strength they can make up for in style and grace.

Many a wife has put her husband to shame by following one of his wild wobbly heaves with a picture-perfect end-over-end toss into a lateral hazard. I say go for it ladies!

Q. How soon should I have my kids start throwing their golf clubs?

A. At Club Throwers of America it's our belief that kids are bearers of the club throwing torch. The future of club tossing in this nation is in our golfing youth. If your kids are old enough to play, they're old enough to throw clubs.

Kids have an advantage over us old folks in that they have yet to develop good habits and good manners. Throwing clubs in anger and having tantrums in public comes naturally to most kids and you'll probably find that they respond enthusiastically to your efforts to guide them in our wonderful pastime.

Q. Don't many golf courses frown on club throwing?

A. It's true that many clubs still discourage the healthy release of anger that comes from lofting a club or two skyward. But we've made great strides in recent years and we hope that soon every golf course will be open to the proud and happy club thrower.

Let's Work Out!

Club throwing, like any strenuous activity, requires that you be in good shape to perform at your peak. With that in mind, we have created an exercise program that combines the principals of muscle development and aerobic fitness especially for the club thrower who wishes to increase his enjoyment of the sport.

Do this workout every other day and you'll soon see your clubs reach new heights and distances. You may be tempted to skip workouts at times. The excuses are endless. It takes too much time, you don't have any place to do it, your wife has already threatened to leave you if you break anything else in the house with a golf club, etc.

But remember, the short time you spend getting and staying shape will pay off ten-fold on the course. So stick to it!

The Two-Iron Twist

1. Begin this warm up exercise with a two-iron held high over your head. Twist slowly to the left, keeping arms fully extended.

2. Make about a 90 degree turn. Then twist back to your start position and continue until you reach about a 90 degree turn to the right.

Do 12 reps, rest one minute, then do 12 more.

The Rail Splitter

Just like old Honest Abe you'll want to wield your club like an axe at times. This exercise will work the muscles you'll need.

1. Start with the club head on the ground, arms extended in front of you. Draw the club back directly over your head, as far as you can.

2. Bring your club back over head and to your starting position.

Do 12 reps, rest one minute, do 12 reps again.

The Hammer Throw

1.   Begin this exercise in the same position as *The Rail Splitter*. Spin slowly in a circle, again holding the club at a full arm's length.

2.   Allow centrifugal force to raise the club up to about eye level as you spin faster and faster.

Do this exercise for 5 minutes or until you fall down.

The O.B. Hop

This is one you can do on the course while waiting for the other members in your group to hit. It's great aerobically and it will come in handy when sneaking over the out of bounds fence to find wayward clubs.

1. Grasp the top of a fence rail. Using your hands for balance, throw both legs over to the other side.

2. Repeat this action in reverse.

Do 3 sets of 10 reps each.

The Scythe

Great for the man who wants to carve out his own space.

1. Swing club side to side extending as far each way as you can.

Do 3 sets of 10 reps each.

Lady Launcher

New from Airborne Golf Clubs comes the *Lady Launcher* series. These extra-light graphite shafted clubs are made for a woman's unique abilities and style. Handcrafted at our factory in Swampgrass, Florida, these cavity backed irons and metal woods will fly farther than you ever thought possible. You may not even want to heave your clubs from the ladies tees anymore!

With your choice of pink, lavender or sky blue grips and matching complimentary head covers. Try a set today!

Airborne Golf Clubs

U.S. Patent 6,678,045

Ante Up!

For many players the enjoyment of a round of golf, and the ensuing mayhem created by flying clubs, is heightened by a bit of wagering.

Betting on the golf course is a long standing tradition among players and betting on club tossing is fast becoming as fashionable and fun as betting on the score.

Following are a few betting games which will increase your enjoyment of the game, focus your concentration, hone your competitive edge and keep your club throwing skills sharp.

THE SCOTCH GAME

This is a partner game in which players score points for throwing their clubs for distance and accuracy. A typical match might have six points available on each hole; two for the most throws, two for the

longest heaves and two for whoever imbeds his club in the green closest to the pin.

THE NASSAU

This traditional bet awards a set amount of money ($2, $10, $100?) for most club throws on the front nine, most on the back nine and most for the overall eighteen. There are numerous variations on the Nassau and players may include rules about how often they may "press", or double the bet, and what kind of "presses" are permitted.

One favorite twist on this game is the "flying press" in which players are allowed to double the bet while the club is in the air and may offer side bets on where it will land, how many pieces it will break in to, whether it will cause property damage and on the total dollar amount of that damage.

Some players play The Lawsuit game and place wagers on the amount of damages an injured golfer can collect from a club thrower or how much he'll settle for out of court. The variations are endless.

THE HORSE RACE

This is an individual game in which an unlimited number of players start at the first hole and play until they throw a club. Players who throw a club must drop out and the last player left collects all the loot. It's sort of like golf course musical chairs.

THE SKINS GAME

In this game, each hole is worth a set amount and players play as individuals against the other members of the group. If two players tie on a hole, everyone ties the hole and the skin carries over to the next hole. For example, if player A throws three clubs on a hole and no one else throws a club more than twice, player A wins the hole. However if Player A throws two clubs and Player B throws two clubs, the hole is tied and the skin carries over, even if Players C and D don't throw any clubs at all.

Getting Really Teed Off!

Throwing that first club on each hole can really set the tone for the day. A player who strides confidently forward and launches his driver straight down the fairway can march down the middle and proudly scoop up what's left of his club before continuing play, comfortable in the knowledge that he's gotten off on the right foot. If your first toss is a shaky one that barely clears the ladies' tee, you may spend the rest of the round trying to recover.

The key to getting off to a good club-throwing start is a solid twenty minute warm-up session. Start by throwing a few putters. Move to the chipping and pitching area and toss a few wedges around. Throw some clubs from the practice sand trap if your driving range has one. Then move to the range and try some full throws, first with the short irons and then working your way up to the woods. This will get you off on the right foot every time!

GRIP RIGHT WITH GRIP-TITE!

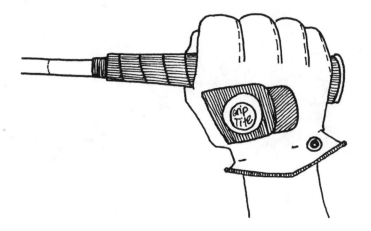

Grip-Tite gloves are the only golf glove designed exclusively
with the club thrower in mind. Our patented two-layer
construction and high-quality Cabretta leather make these
gloves ideal in all playing conditions. They'll give you
the sure grip you need to launch your
clubs with deadly accuracy!

Grip-Tite Gloves

The 20 Basic Throws

To be a truly successful club thrower you must master the 20 Basic Throws. Each of which is described and illustrated in the following pages. Make these tosses part of your regular practice and soon you'll be the envy of all your playing partners. And, in addition, you'll have the basis for inventing and perfecting your own club throws and developing your own club throwing style.

Each of the basic tosses is shown here with a little club tossing poem which you should memorize. This is a mnemonic device (like Every Good Boy Does Fine, for instance) which will help you to remember, in the heat of your club throwing passion, the correct throw for each situation that you find yourself in.

Once you have committed these to memory you'll be on your way to a new and much more fulfilling club throwing career!

The Whirlybird

It soars so gently
through the air,
Like a chopper in the blue,
You fling your club
with style and flair,
Because you are a chopper, too.

This is the classic toss. Use the basic method as described in chapter 2. This is appropriate in almost all club throwing situations, especially on the first and tenth tee when you'll have spectators and will want to look your best.

The Rainmaker

Cumulus-nimbi &
thunderheads,
May have a silver lining,
But go to any Nineteenth hole,
And you'll hear
some real whining.

Again, this is a classic. Start with the clubhead on the ground, arms extended in front of you. Squat down until your thighs are approximately parallel to the ground. Then spring upward and thrust your club skyward. Remember to follow through completely. And to duck!

Fling!

The Tree Coil

A putter you will oft times see,
Stuck high up in a favorite tree,
But strange as though I've
always found it,
You'll sometimes see one
wrapped around it.

This is especially good when you've just tried a
miracle shot you had no business trying and your ball
has hit a tree and has actually gone deeper into the
woods than it was before. Get a full shoulder turn
and hit the tree about halfway up the shaft and it
should bend around the trunk nicely. Or, it could
shatter into a thousand pieces, and that's nice, too.

The Scraper

Ruin in a fit of rage,
A wood on which for years you've doted,
And later you may rue the fact,
That golf clubs are not
Teflon coated.

Sometimes you'll just want to drag the sucker on the ground for awhile. This can be fun because there are so many interesting surfaces available to do damage to your golf clubs. Try the easy access cart path for starters, the sidewalk by the clubhouse or the gravel parking lot. If you're really ticked off, you can tie one to the bumper for the ride home.

The Tee Plant

Like Johnny with his apple seeds,
You pound your tees in everywhere,
Perhaps you'll drive one deep enough,
That a tee tree will grow there.

Sometimes, just for a change of pace, you'll want to take your anger out on something other than your clubs. One of the most satisfying ways to vent your spleen is to pound your tee into the turf until it disappears. There are tees now available on the market made of fertilizer which are actually good for the grass. Just the excuse you need to use this club "throw."

The Javelin Toss

Before you heave a club this way,
Please warm up first
and do your stretching,
You'd rather do the javelin throw,
Than try to do the javelin catching.

Good form is the key to this stylish toss.
Imagine an Olympic decathlete as you get your
running start. After about a twenty or thirty yard
sprint, turn sideways holding your club like a javelin,
grip forward. Plant your left foot and fling the club
up and out using hips, shoulders and legs for power.
With practice you'll be able to stick a two-iron in the
turf like a headhunter's spear.

The Oil Well

Four tries and still you're in the sand,
Your teeth may grit, your blood may boil,
But look upon the brighter side,
You're very close to striking oil!

The key here is to use your sand wedge to get as much sand as you can out of the bunker. Happily, this club is made for exactly that, with a high degree of loft and wide flange. A determined club thrower can empty an average sized greenside bunker in ten minutes flat.

The Hankie Drop

Coquetteishly you drop your club,
Though you'd rather let it fly,
You're certainly a gentleman,
When the ranger is nearby.

Sadly, many clubs still frown on club tossing. Some places will even ask you to leave if you attempt to practice this fine art. Should you find yourself at one of these behind-the-times joints you may have to content yourself with this genteel little toss. Until the ranger takes off anyway.

The Spike

Football players celebrate,
When they go in for six,
They slam the ball down
just the way you,
Slam your useless sticks.

Be as creative as you like on this one! Go behind the back, between the legs or slam dunk over a nearby tree. Throw in a little Deion Sanders touchdown dance.

The Over The Shoulder

Casually you toss your club,
But forget to look behind you,
A partner, though,
may find a way,
To painfully remind you.

When going for club throwing "style" points it can be tempting to fling one over your shoulder without looking. Unfortunately, this little habit can result in injuries and lawsuits. So look before you heave!

The Ubangi Stomp

The tantrums that you often throw,
Are like an ancient tribal dance,
You lack face paint and feathers but,
At least you have the pants.

Ugly pants have always had a place in the game of golf and they can really enhance your enjoyment of this little tantrum. When you miss a little putt it's fun to high step around the hole in agony, screaming an unintelligible string of curses and gibberish in a high, wailing voice. This has the added benefit of tearing up the green for the people in your group who still have to putt out.

The Twist

You three putt for the seventh time,
It may never stop,
Your putter's like an ice cold beer,
With a twist-off top.

Three (and four) putting is a great reason to mangle your equipment. Since most club throwers have well developed wrists and forearms from those twist-off beer caps, popping a putter head or two should be no problem.

The Roof Shot

The condo owner won't return,
The putter he found on his roof,
Golf is not the game you play,
The game you play is goof.

During your club throwing career you'll find that it's tempting to fire a club or two O.B. There is something undeniably pleasing about a well thrown golf club hurtling over a fence and disappearing. The resulting crash and cry of anger and pain can be amusing too.

The Trespasser

You climbed the fence in search of clubs,
You tossed into the morning fog,
You never saw that backyard sign,
The one that said
"Beware of Dog."

Lots of people who bought golf course property for the peace and quiet, have found themselves living under siege. They may be less than understanding about your club throwing needs. In this case it's best to let sleeping dogs lie.

The Swashbuckler

Gallahad and knights of old,
Were gallant swordsmen just like you,
Woe unto a laughing caddie,
'Cause you might run that sucker
through.

Many caddies have developed a less than reverent attitude toward club throwers. It is important to keep these youngsters in line for your sake and for your club throwing brothers who may have to deal with the insolent wretches later.

The Repeater

Thrice you try a three foot putt,
For par, and thrice you rim it,
Too bad the rules of golf enforce,
A strict fourteen club limit.

As you develop your club heaving you'll want to add speed to your arsenal of skills to go along with distance and accuracy. Practice at the range and see how fast you can empty a bag of golf clubs. Some advanced club tossers get to where they throw with both hands!

The Swizzle Stick

The poolside guest may be upset,
He may cause quite a stink,
If that club you lofted came,
To rest within his drink.

Target tossing can be loads of fun. And golf course targets are plentiful, especially along the ninth and eighteenth. Firing a putter into the pool, clubhouse or tennis courts can bring true club heaving pleasure, as well as bills for damages. But that's the price you pay for having so darn much fun.

The Caddie-Killer

Heavy bags and flying clubs,
Make jocking less than super,
They're the hazards occupational,
In the life of every looper

Hey, these kids get paid well. They need to be on their toes! If you should accidentally spear a slow-moving caddy with a flying four wood it's his problem. Club throwing etiquette does require that you double the tip for any caddy who ends up needing emergency room treatment.

The Speed Bump

Tossing one's clubs,
One by one is an art,
But to efficiently wreck them,
You must use a cart.

Sometimes you just want to smash all your clubs to pieces and go to the bar. That's why it important to practice this key club "toss." Don't just run your bag over. Back your cart up and get up a good head of steam. Tip one of the clubhouse boys to get you one of the souped up carts they use to tear around the course. And don't forget to back up over your clubs a few times too. For good measure.

The Ice Fisher

In the blust'ry winter cold,
The golfer plays undaunted,
Though his presence on the ice,
May oft times be unwanted.

As a dedicated club thrower you must practice your art even in very difficult conditions. Throw your clubs in the Spring. Throw them in the Summer, Fall and Winter, too. Throw them at the public course and at the private country club. Throw them in the rain, sleet, snow and in the hot sunshine. Throw them where ever and when ever the mood strikes, but what ever you do, throw them!

You Know You're A Club Thrower If...

1. The club repair guy refers to you as "The Franchise."

2. Your regular caddy wears a hockey helmet.

3. When you reach into your bag to select a club your playing partners dive for cover.

4. You have learned to putt with every other club in your bag "just in case."

5. You carry duct tape and Crazy Glue in your bag.

6. Your homeowner's insurance company has you in your own separate risk pool.

7. You are deluged with business cards from personal injury attorneys whenever you play.

8. You have developed "carpal tunnel syndrome" from your repetitive throwing motion.

9. Your local course now demands that you leave a security deposit along with green fees.

10. Like Michael Jordan, your nickname is "Air."

Tom Carey is a writer/illustrator from
Chicago. His previously published
work includes
*The Modern Guide To Sex Etiquette, Too!,
Teed Off!* and *The Marriage Dictionary*.

He plays golf all the time and only breaks a club
if it really, really deserves it.

Also available from
Double Eagle Press:

The Marriage Dictionary	$ 6.95
The I Love To Fart Diet	$ 6.95
The Modern Guide To Sex, Too!	$ 7.95
Teed Off! A Modern Guide To Golf	$ 7.95
The Club Thrower's Handbook	$ 9.95
Your Baby: An Owner's Manual	$ 7.95
Baby's 40th Birthday Book	$10.95

Double Eagle Press
books are distributed through
Sourcebooks, Inc.
1-800-SBS-8866